Emily Alston

And the White Snow Falls All Around

A cumulative Christmas poem
based on the folk song
"The Green Grass Grows All Around"

And the White Snow Falls All Around

Emily Alston

Oh in the night,
There was a mountain,
The prettiest mountain
that you ever did see.

Oh the mountain in the night,
And the white snow falls
around and around,

And the white snow falls all round.

And in that mountain,
There was a valley,
The pretties valley that you ever did see.

Oh the valley in the mountain,
And the mountain in the night,
And the white snow falls
around and around,

And the white snow falls all round.

And in that valley,
There was a town,
The prettiest town that you ever did see.

Oh the town in the valley,
And the valley in the mountain,
And the mountain in the night,
And the white snow falls
around and around,
And the white snow falls all round.

And in that town,
There was a house,
The prettiest house that you ever did see.

Oh the house in the town,
And the town in the valley,
And the valley in the mountain,
And the mountain in the night,
And the white snow falls
around and around,

And the white snow falls all round.

And on that house,
There was a roof,
The prettiest roof that you ever did see.

Oh the roof on the house,
And the house in the town,
And the town in the valley,
And the valley in the mountain,
And the mountain in the night,
And the white snow falls
around and around,

And the white snow falls all round.

And on that roof,
There was a sled,
The prettiest sled
that you ever did see.

Oh the sled on the roof,
And the roof on the house,
And the house in the town,
And the town in the valley,
And the valley in the mountain,
And the mountain in the night,
And the white snow falls
around and around,

And the white snow falls all round.

And on that sled,
There was a sack,
The prettiest sack that you ever did see.

Oh the sack on the sled,
the sled on the roof,
And the roof on the house,
And the house in the town,
And the town in the valley,
And the valley in the mountain,
And the mountain in the night,
And the white snow falls
around and around,

And the white snow falls all round.

And in that sack,
There was a box,
The biggest box that you ever did see.

Oh the box in the sack,
And the sack on the sled,
And the sled on the roof,
And the roof on the house,
And the house in the town,
And the town in the valley,
And the valley in the mountain,
And the mountain in the night,
And the white snow falls
around and around,
And the white snow falls all round.

And in that box,
There was a toy,
The coolest toy that you ever did see.

Oh the toy in the box,
And the box in the sack,
And the sack on the sled,
And the sled on the roof,
And the roof on the house,
And the house in the town,
And the town in the valley,
And the valley in the mountain,
And the mountain in the night,
And the white snow falls around and around,

And the white snow falls all round.

A Poem for Every Holiday

If you liked this book, discover other holiday books
in this series by Emily Alston.

Each book is a holiday-themed retelling of the favorite
kids' folk song "*And the Green Grass Grows All Around*".
Kids will recognize the pattern of these cumulative verses
and will be singing along to the books in no time.

HALLOWEEN

THANKSGIVING

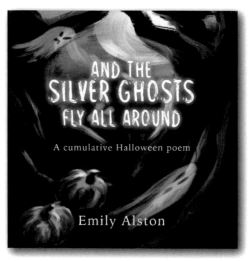

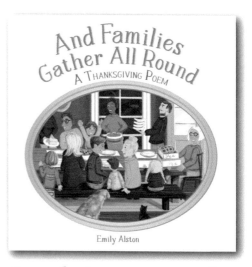

Search Amazon.com for
ASIN: B08KH3T5X2

Search Amazon.com for
ASIN: B08M7NK8F6

Fully hand-illustrated by independent artist and author
Emily Alston.

Upcoming publications:
Valentine's Day, Easter and Mother's Day

Made in the USA
Las Vegas, NV
26 November 2023

81588239R00026